Apocalypse Journal

I0451912

Days 1-100

Martin Tiller

"Just me, the kid, and the apocalypse..."

Author's Facebook post

ISBN: 978-0-9996879-4-9

Dedication

To Rachel:

Glad to be your dad. The school said you were gifted. But you have gifted me.

Table of Contents

Apocalypse Journal

Days 1-100

Journal Entry: Apocalypse Day 1

The eight year old had a meltdown due to the fact her teacher sent homework via email, and her father could access said email and understand Google Classroom.

The eight year old had a friend over, inspite of the social pressure to not have friends over, because the friend's mother is out vanquishing zombies. And she needed childcare.

I spent the morning cleaning the bunker. Every clean spot I considered a victory.

We took a brief respite outside, as it unwise to let the canine relieve herself inside the bunker. We saw two other children who quickly scurried behind a tree. Several vultures flew over head. But they avoided us-- today.

Back inside the eight year and friend have not yet caused chaos. But it is early.

The pop tarts rations are supposed to arrive tomorrow. This keeps me going.

Day 2

The eight year old woke me early, telling me she had a nightmare. I let her sleep on my side of the bunker. I didn't have the stomach to tell her it wasn't a nightmare. It was Tuesday.

The eight year old was better behaved today getting her work done from her teacher. That maybe because her friend was not able to be with us today. I fear she may have been eaten by zombies.

Last evening I found an unopened bag of Starbucks coffee. I've never felt such wealth. Unsure if I am going to trade it for gasoline, shotgun shells, or toilet paper. Or if I am going to keep it for when the zombies are defeated, and I sit outside my bunker drinking its dark, bitter life giving taste like a king over a small kingdom.

The kid and I took our daily respite and walked the canine. In honor of her teacher we practiced her math skills by counting the number of tumbleweeds we saw.

And by reviewing word problems, "How many

wings total do four vultures have?"

"Depends on what they're eating," she replied.

Smart.

She's going to need that skill against the zombies.

I came home and saw that other hermits had shared color coded schedules for their bunker.

That's cute.

But zombies don't care about your color coded excel spreadsheet.

They come at any time.

Night

Morning

Self-Sustained Reading

Doesn't matter the time.

I received unsettling news today.

The pop tart rations won't be replenished for another two days. The wine supply seems to okay. I just pray it will last until the pop tarts arrive.

Day 3

The eight year old said she got scared again and needed to sleep on my side of the bunker. I'm beginning to think she just like my bigger bunk. Note to self: Lock door.

During our daily respite with the canine we saw another child, but she scampered away back to her bunker when she saw us.

We practiced math facts for her teacher by skip counting the tumbleweeds we saw.

Later in the afternoon, I heard the eight year old outside. She was talking with Crazy Carl. I stepped outside and Carl hid behind his jeep. It was clear he was attaching a flamethrower to the back of his jeep. I had to remind the eight year old, we leave Crazy Carl alone.

Second Note to self--trade coffee for flamethrower and fire extinguisher.

Then out on the horizon a transport appeared. It pulled in front of the bunker and a man got out, covered in black goggles, and overalls. He told me his name was Bill and he had package for me. He gave me the package and drove off into the dusty sunset.

I opened the box. It was the pop tart rations. A day early.

Thank the Good Lord for Bill. He saved the world today.

Day 4

Short update as streaming is currently working. Not sure if the zombies will kill streaming.

Killed wasps around the bunker. Afraid wasps may thrive in the time of zombies.

To celebrate the killings I broke out the rations.

Enjoyed Pop tarts and wine.

Day 5

Had to wash the canine today. Fleas are huge during this time of zombies. I am confused to why they are size of grapes.

The eight year old sent a writing assignment to her teacher. The teacher replied, "I'm going to need more details."

Aren't we all teacher...aren't we all.

Afterwards made the eight year old expand our "garden" by digging several more feet and planted vegetable seeds. After seeing the fleas, I am worried about what may come out of the ground. The cucumbers may bite.

Saw Crazy Carl still working on his flame thrower. Which reminds me, exchange toilet paper for a fire extinguisher, and dig a moat.

I've decided not to exchange my coffee. Even during the apocalypse, one must keep their manners up.

So far the pop tart rations and wine supply are holding. This gives me hope.

Day 6

Had to clean the bunker today. The eight year old was not happy about it. Lots of whining. Unfortunately, I didn't see a zombie outside to take her though.

Took the canine for a walk, the buzzards seemed to be getting closer.

We saw no other children. Afraid the zombies have eaten them.

Later wrapped ourselves in goggles and masks, got into the transport, and headed to get provisions.

Got Sangria--it was a successful trip.

Day 7

The calendar says seven days. My body says it's been 14 years.

There is a groundhog near our bunker. I was informed animals can't be zombies. But this guy is enormous. Has to be a zombie--or alien.

I believe we walked the canine four times today. The canine is living her best life.

The eight year old communicated with her cousins for several hours today. Thank the Good Lord, the zombies haven't eliminated the internet--yet.

We broke out a puzzle today.

Which means I need to breakout the pop tart and wine rations.

Day 8

The zombies took the school today. That's a tough loss. Some people didn't believe it. I tried to warn them. Zombies can come at anytime.

I told the eight year old the news. I was surprised when, she jumped up and down with excitement.

We'll see how excited she is with tomorrow's list of homework and chores.

Because the bunker ain't gonna clean itself.

Checking my rations, there's not enough pop tarts to deal with this loss.

Day 9

We're falling into a routine here. There is less whining.

Expect during multiplication fact practice. Then there is enough whining to make me want to BE a zombie.

Several kids were out today playing in the street. Hard to tell if they were zombies.

Didn't want to be in the position to have to take them out in front of their parents. So we just stayed away.

Tried to order educational supplies today for the eight year old. But it would take nearly a month to get them. Now not only have the zombies taken the school, they've taken the school supplies chain as well. The zombies maybe winning.

But I still have Sangria rations--so they haven't won yet.

Day 10

It rained today. It washed away the sand and dust, and kept the zombie children inside.

Me and the eight-year-old went into town to get provisions--we were short on cheese sticks and cookies.

We wrapped ourselves in our black goggles, black gloves, and wrapped our faces in scarfs. The outfit helps with "social distancing."

It helps when saying things like, "I need you to put one package of toilet paper back. I clearly see you have two--Karen."

Or this exchange "I need you to step back."

"Oh, are you one of those 'Social Distance' people. I'm not sick."

"Yeah, But I might be."

She stepped back.

Thanks--Karen.

And finally, "I'm going to need you to not take take the last bottle of Sangria--Karen."

It's a very useful outfit.

Day 11

The eight-year-old seems to be getting used to the idea of school at home. We'll see when the teacher stops reviewing and starts teaching new things. At least she can be in her PJs in the bunker while learning about simple machines and adding with decimals.

Once she learns about simple machines, will she be able to help change the oil in the transport? Or change a tire? Or is that on me?

The days are starting to blur together--is it Friday? Monday? Christmas? Easter?

The-eight-year-old asked when the last day of school was. I told her June 12.

Which makes me wonder, can tomorrow be June 12?

Day 12

The weather was warmer today. More people out. Or more zombies. You just don't know which.

So you keep your eyes on them. And keep your distance.

Crazy Carl was out working on his flame thrower. You keep your distance from Carl just because he's crazy.

I don't think the eight-year-old did all of her school work today.

Afraid she may have figured out the loophole of no grading.

That's fine. The chore list can increase. This bunker and the canine aren't going to clean themselves.

Day 13

Day 13? Can't be, I could have sworn it was year 3.

It's getting warmer. I saw tumbleweed today with blossoms. I didn't know they could do that. Maybe it has something to do with the zombies.

The internet is something about a Tiger King. So I decided to see what the fuss was about--and clearly the zombies have won.

It's time to hunker down and borrow the flame thrower from Crazy Carl.

On the other hand, my pop tarts and sangria rations are doing well. That's what gets me through.

Day 14

I ventured out today to check the lawn around the bunker. Luckily the sand from desert as not encroached onto the lawn yet.

I was told that animals don't become zombies. But I jumped a country mile when a snake appeared beside my feet. In the times, before the zombies, it would have been referred to as a black snake.

But today it was the biggest darn thing I've ever seen. Seven. eight, nine feet at least.

First the huge ground hog and now this Gozilla reptile in my lawn.

Animals can't be zombies--my butt.

I may talk to Crazy Carl about torching my lawn.

Day 15

The eight year old had her first school class video conference.

Get used to it kid, that's how all human interaction will be from now on.

The zombies are winning. Food is getting low. I would assume that means it's Monday. But it could be a Thursday in May of the year 2045 and I wouldn't know the difference.

So to get provisions I have to begin preparing to leave the bunker. I have goggles, gloves, face mask all lined up at the door. Crazy Carl's flamethrower is in the back of the transport--and shopping list.

We're not sure how to beat the zombies.

But here I think we're all on the same page,

Carol definitely killed her husband.

Day 16

The eight-year-old had another nightmare and slept on my side of the bunker. I asked her what it was about. Something about a dead horse. I wonder if she saw our ground hog and confused it with a horse.

It was cold and rainy today. In theory that should wash away the sand and pollen, as it did in The Days Before. But now in the Time of Zombies it does not.

The teacher met with the eight year old over an online video call. The call lasted for one hour.

In The Days Before, teacher, you met with her for six hours. I'm gonna need a six hour phone call tomorrow.

We gathered supplies today. Fewer people today. I hope the zombies didn't get them. But we did replenish the cookie rations, so that was a bright side.

Day 17

The eight year old slept on my side of the bunker again. I give up. The four Pokemon of the Apocalypse she sleeps with apparently isn't enough.

I missed the trash transport today. I have no idea what day it is.

I hope that doesn't come back to bite me--like the Godzilla snake that is in my yard.

It would be one thing to go by zombie in the apocalypse, but to go by drowning in trash is another--and not how one would want to go.

If the pile gets too big, I'll trade some coffee with Crazy Carl to torch the trash.

Day 18

Crap. The Pop tart rations are low. So I need to put the goggles, gloves, and mask next to the door--need to travel tomorrow.

Is all that preparation worth it? Or should I just let the zombies just take me?

What day is it? In The Time Before, I think this would have been a Friday. A day of importance, I believe. Now in The Time of Zombies, it's just another tally mark on the wall.

The trash pile isn't growing so that's good news. And the sangria rations are okay. That'll get me through a few more tally marks.

Day 18

[Author's note. I know I repeat Day 18. I catch up a few days later. I'm leaving it the way I originally wrote it.]

We were told the enemy is the zombies. But maybe it's the boredom of waiting for the throng of zombies to come running over the hill. Maybe that's the enemy, the boredom.

So I put on my running shoes, my black goggles, and a mask and took a jog around the neighborhood. Wanted to check out the other bunkers. Except for the growing number of tumbleweeds--the streets were empty. Those people that were out were polite enough to step to the side.

Except for a vulture that landed in the middle of the street, and wouldn't move. That vulture is definitely a zombie.

My trash pile didn't get bigger today. Crazy Carl will have to wait on his trash bonfire.

Day 19

The eight year old got up at 6:50 AM. I have no idea why. Something about getting up early to get to do more fun things. I want to live in that timeline.

In The Days Before,I believe this would have been Saturday--which would have been cleaning day and yard work day. But now in the Days of Zombies we got exactly zero cleaning and yard work done today. Zero.

But that is a good way to avoid the Godzilla snake and King Kong ground hog in my yard.

Except I did move the trash container to the road. Not missing that again, even if it is several more tally marks on the wall away.

Made the eight year old get into the transport so we could get more food rations. Still no toilet paper but we're good on that for awhile, but they had Pop tarts. So we live another day.

Day 20

Got news today a tiger has become a zombie. Nobody believes me about my Godzllla snake and King Kong ground hog. But they'll believe a tiger can become a zombie.

We ventured out several times today to let the canine relieve herself outside. The vultures are getting closer. And the tumbleweeds have blossoms. That's new.

The eight-years-old teacher said she won't be meeting with her this week. Something about Spring Break. Wait. What?

In The Time Before it may have been referred to as Spring Break, but in the Time of Zombies, well I don't know what to call. Teacher I need you. Please call her tomorrow.

Teacher--you can have a pop tart and a sangria. Just set up a Zoom meeting.

Day 21

How the heck has it been three weeks? If feels like a decade in this bunker.

I'm concerned about the animals. The eight year old saw a lizard in the bunker. I had to get it out, and then show her it was fine. The lizard didn't seem to be a zombie.

Questions--Was it moving in because it's running from zombies, or was it a zombie and I just didn't know it? Are the zombies adapting?

The eight year old is also afraid of mosquitoes. Now in The Time Before, mosquitoes would be something to not be afraid of. And now in The Time of Zombies, I still try to teach her mosquitoes aren't something to be afraid of. But I maybe lying. She pointed to one by the door of the bunker, I swatted it, and I swear on all the Pop Tarts--it swatted back.

I'm at least not worried about the canine. She just sleeps all day and gets up twice a day to poop by the tumbleweeds. I don't think she knows it's The Time of Zombies.

The sangria rations may need replenishing soon. But there's enough for tonight. That's a nice way to celebrate a decade in the bunker.

Day 22

The eight-year-old's teacher still hasn't called. I hope the zombies haven't gotten her.

Luckily the eight-year-old seems pretty smart, she's on her laptop a lot anyway. Maybe she's coming up with a way to stop the zombies. At least that's what she told me.

We took the canine out to relieve herself. The vultures seem to be getting bigger--or closer.

I asked the eight-year-old, since this is technically Spring Break, what would she want to do if this was The Time Before. She said something about a "Water Park." I don't even remember what that is.

The trash container has been out by the road for several days. I hope the zombies didn't get the trash guys. I don't want to die by trash pile.

Maybe Crazy Carl will get to use his flamethrower after all.

Day 23

The stir crazy maybe kicking in here. Looking at the same bunker everyday is getting tough. I almost wish the zombies would just full on attack, it's the waiting that's killing us.

Plus it would be interesting to see Crazy Carl in action.

The trash was picked up this morning. So won't die this week from a huge pile of trash. But I do need to replenish the Pop Tarts. May die if that isn't attended too.

The eight-year-old spent a lot of time on the laptop today. She still hasn't solved the zombie issue yet. Not sure how much longer she is going to need.

Need to get the mask, and gloves by the door. May need to make a Pop Tart run tomorrow.

Day 24

The weather is getting better. But the mosquitoes are as big as birds now--so not sure how we're going to survive summer.

A darn salesman came to bunker today. I was so mad, I pointed my blaster right at his forehead.

"Whoa! Man I'm not a zombie!" he screamed.

"Yeah, but I might be! And I'm Han shot first kinda guy!"

He got the message. He ran as fast as his heavily protected legs could go. He looked like Buster Keaton in an old black and white silent film.

I came back in and realized the Sangria rations will need to be replenished soon. Luckily I found a white wine as back up.

But let's be honest, white wine isn't really a zombie apocalypse pairing.

This is slowly becoming more a Bourbon or whiskey appropriate apocalypse.

Day 25

It got colder today. That's concerning, zombies apparently do better in the cold.

Despite the cold and Zombie supporting weather, the eight-year-old and I ventured out of the bunker--the boredom was palatable.

At least with the cold the mosquito-birds weren't out as much.

But the vultures were and they seemed to be getting--bolder. Landing and walking twenty feet in front of us--smelling us and then flying away. That can't be good.

On a more hopeful note the eight-year-old's teacher should be calling back in a few days. Please teacher, don't ever stop calling again. I'll send pop tarts--or whiskey.

Day 26

Trimmed the lawn today. No Godzilla Snake or King Kong Ground Hog seen today. But they're there... they're there.

Battling the stir crazy, I put on my goggles and mask and explored the neighborhood. Tumbleweed blew across the road. I noticed pollen now looks like sand. It's large, heavy, and rain doesn't wash it away-- Zombie Pollen.

I discovered today that pirates have gotten hold of the last known stash of Pop Tarts and are jacking up the prices.

Crap, now I'm at war with pirates and zombies.

And shoot, that's means Crazy Carl and his Jeep Flamethrower and me may need to team up.

It's official--this is now a whiskey apocalypse.

Day 27

I noticed I am sort of becoming a zoologist for this time of zombies. In the southern part of my land I noticed, what would have been referred to in The Time Before, a duck. Now in the Time of Zombies, a more appropriate name would be a Pterodactyl.

A house fly would keep it's name, because it is now the size of a house.

Tomorrow the eight-year-old's teacher is supposed to call. Alleluia! She will return.

In other news, I heard reports of a bad storm coming, so I began preparing the bunker. I now have to fight the weather, pirates, and zombies.

Gonna need to stock up on the Pop Tarts--and whiskey. Yes, the whiskey.

Day 29

Looking through this journal I realize I had miscounted. I had two day 18s. A ground hog day I guess. Or in this case a King Kong Ground Hog Day.

The calendar says a month and day. My brain says a decade and eight months and sixteen days.

To keep the crazy at bay did some major cleaning of the bunker today. Every inch clean I considered a victory. It maybe the only victory I get for awhile.

The storms sent a huge amount of rain down today, and the wind threaten to blow the bunker over. But we survived. I think I saw a tuna swim by at one point.

In spite of the rain, pollen is still everywhere--Zombie pollen.

Now it's time to turn in and pray the Sangria rations are holding.

Day 30

Thirty days, that's a lot of tally marks on the wall of the bunker.

The eight-year-old complained about school. I reminded her in The Time Before she couldn't go to school in her pajamas with no shoes on a daily basis, so she could be thankful for that. Or she could go outside to trap the Godzilla Snake--She chose to learn about main idea instead.

Her teacher did call back. I threw out any self-respect and begged her to not leave me again. Just tell me where to send the paper towels, pop tarts, and whiskey.

The eight-year-old reminded me to put the trash container to the road. So she helped avoid a catastrophe. So I'll keep her for today.

I replenished the sangria rations today. I can survive another tally mark on the wall.

Day 31

Had to get out the generator today. The zombies cut the power at 4:45 in the morning. They're getting smart.

When they cut the power we put on our masks and gloves and went out to get coffee. Even during the apocalypse we need fuel--both gasoline and coffee.

Unfortunately, The eight-year-old nearly blew up the bunker with her boredom. So I have to watch out for zombies and an eight-year-old.

Thank goodness we got the power back on in time for her call with her teacher. Don't ever leave again--power or teacher.

While outside repairing the electricity, I did hear what was referred to, in The Time Before, as an owl. From what I heard, I believe, now in The Time of Zombies, they shall be referred to as Dragons.

Now where's that whiskey.

Day 32

It's supposed to cold tonight. That's bad zombies, like the cold. In The Time Before this was called April. Yet there is a freeze warning, in April--Zombie weather.

In the market today, I noticed face-gear is getting pretty. Nice designs, different fabrics, floral, cute.

Zombies don't give a King Kong Ground Hog Butt about the design of your face-gear. Just make sure it works. It needs to keep out zombie breath, zombie pollen, and the smoke from Crazy Carl's flamethrower. Flowers aren't gonna cut it.

And you think clear lunch lady gloves are gonna protect you from zombie pollen? Good luck. We're keeping our black leather gloves. When I finally get that Godzilla Snake, grabbing it with clear plastic gloves that used to pass out square lunch pizzas to ten-year-olds, well that wouldn't end well for me. I'll keep my leather gloves.

It's getting cold--time to visit the whiskey rations.

Day 33

We survived the cold night. But the Zombies are getting closer.

Luckily we have enough pop tarts and sangria to last awhile.

Because I had to travel, the eight-year-old stayed the day with a friend who was assigned to fight zombies from their bunker. I noticed in my travels not everyone has face-gear.

Fine. Hope that works out for you. Hope the Zombie pollen doesn't get up your nose and into your brain--Zombie Brain.

Have to attend to the land around the bunker tomorrow. I am coming for you Godzilla Snake. You scared me once, but I know you're there. I know you're there...

Day 34

It's getting difficult, when you willingly clean the bunker to fight boredom. But every inch cleaned is a victory. I even learned how to change the batteries on an old Swifter Wet Jet--I need every victory right now.

The eight-year-old even helped clean the bunker, but only at night, and only at bedtime, and most certainly not while I was cleaning. The eight-year-old was literally cleaning the latrine as opposed to going to bed--hope she's not a Zombie.

We took the canine outside to relieve herself, not going to let her mess up a clean bunker. While outside we noticed the vultures are getting bolder--closer. May need to ask Crazy Carl to borrow his flamethrower if they get any closer.

Cleaning the bunker, I lined the wall with my old books, some books spoke of zombies, and they were written as entertainment. Oh silly writers...

Day 35

I believe, in The Time Before, this was Sunday.

I lose count with the tally marks on the wall. I just assumed then it was bath night for the eight-year-old. She wastes a lot of soap, and water--that hurts the war effort.

The bunker though is still relatively clean--victory.

The King Kong Ground Hog's hole to his home seems to be covered over with weeds. That doesn't mean he's moved on, probably just setting a trap for us.

I noticed today Crazy Carl seems to be working on a bear trap.

What does he know about zombies that I don't know?

I have extra coffee, maybe I can trade it for the bear trap, and get the King Kong Ground Hog instead.

But assuming I am correct that it's Sunday, then what the heck-- It's Sangria time.

Day 36

36 days. I quiz the eight-year-old that 12x3 equals 36. But let's be honest it feels like 4,000. Math is even different in the Days of Zombies.

The zombies interfered with the internet with the eight-year-olds call with her teacher. She almost gave up on the call. The zombies may be winning.

The eight-year-old didn't even bother to get our of her pajamas for her phone call with her teacher. Pajamas--The New Zombie School Uniform.

Taking the canine out, the canine barked at a kid wearing her face-gear. Gonna need to retrain her on what to bark at. Unless of course the kid is a zombie, never mind--bark at anything that moves.

Especially Crazy Carl he now has a flamethrower and a bear trap.

Day 37

Made a trip to get food. Wore the face-gear. Maybe we wouldn't be dealing with zombies if we had been wearing face-gear the whole time. But in The Time Before, I would have been immediately detained if I wore my level of face-gear to the store.

I saw two dragon ducks fly past my bunker this afternoon. Maybe they killed the King Kong Ground Hog. Maybe they torched him. I wonder if he was crunchy and good with ketchup.

I heard a few pterodactyl owls this evening. Between the pterodactyl owls and dragon ducks, maybe the zombies aren't going to attack from the ground, but the air.

There's not enough pop tart rations for this nonsense.

Day 38

Crazy Carl was screaming today in his bunker. I didn't check on him at first. I was afraid to what I would see. When I did look through the window he was just calmly polishing his bear trap. What is it you know crazy man?

The eight-year-old and I got some exercise today. We noticed just how much clearer the streets were during an apocalypse. Minus of course, the three huge vultures that walked across our path--they're getting bolder.

I noticed though the vultures don't come near the bunker, the dragon ducks must keep them away.

The eight-year-old's video call with her teacher seemed shorter today, I hope that doesn't continue. But then again in The Time of Zombies, who really know how long things last anyway.

38 tally marks on the wall, I see. That calls for a trip to the pop tart and sangria rations.

Day 39

It was a cold and rainy day--Zombie weather.

Ventured a little bit beyond the bunker. The zombie rain does not wash away zombie pollen. Also may have seen a zombie catfish in stream by the bunker. That could be a problem.

Crazy Carl seems to be attaching his flamethrower to a boat. What does he know that I don't?

The eight-year-old never left her pajamas. Not exactly proper attire if the zombies do decide to attack today.

Saw an article today stating that casual alcohol use may cause cancer. Seriously, you're going to publish that now? Read the bunker!

Now it's cold--where's the whiskey?

Day 40

40 Days and 40 nights. This thing is officially Biblical.

The eight-yer-old didn't want to go out of the bunker today because of "wasps."

Wait til I tell her about the dragon ducks, the pterodactyl owls, King Kong Groundhog, or Godzilla snake.

There was a biblical level storm today that came by at 4 pm. About 4 million gallons was dropped in twenty minutes. The should give the Great White Catfish more room to eat.

That must by why Crazy Carl had attached a flamethrower to his boat. He knew the flood was coming. But he's no Noah--The only person getting on that boat, is Carl.

Time to check the rations and hope the sangria and

Pop Tarts didn't float away.

Day 41

It's cold and raining--wonderful. Maybe the zombies will be swimming when they attack.

It's been raining so much that I may need to release a dove when it's over. But if I did that the dragon-ducks would probably eat it--or roast it first then eat it. A crunchy dove for dinner.

The canine doesn't like the zombie rain. Sorry bub--not relieving yourself in the bunker.

There's a story going around saying the bleach kills zombies. That's stupid--everyone knows it's a gunshot to the head. You use the bleach to clean the zombie blood off the clothes.

41 days. That's a lot of tally marks on the wall.

But the sangria and Pop Tart rations are good--so I can make it a few more tally marks.

Day 42

Zombie rain--it's back or really it never left.

But the zombie pollen is still here how is that possible?

I saw one dragon duck chasing two dragon ducks on the southern part of my land, and I wonder what they did to make him mad.

Crazy Carl now has a machine gun next to his flamethrower on his boat. I have concerns.

In The Time Before, tomorrow would be Monday. And in The Time Before I wouldn't care for Mondays, but now in The Time of Zombies, Mondays mean the teacher calls the Eight-Year-Old. I have missed you teacher...

With 40 days of zombies and 40 days of rain, sangria ain't gonna cut it--I guess whiskey it is then.

Day 43

Complete with face-gear went to the market today. Not everyone is wearing face-gear. Good luck being a zombie. Hope that works out for you. Can I have your bunker?

It stopped raining today. Maybe I should release a zombie dove. Maybe it'll bring back a zombie cure. Or whiskey--same thing.

The eight-year-olds teacher mentioned I hadn't signed up for a phone call. I don't need her calling me, just keep calling the eight-year-old everyday.

Crap, just realized I forgot to replenish the Pop Tart rations. I guess I need to put the face-gear next to the door for another excursion tomorrow.

At least the Sangria rations are good.

Day 44

Holy Crap, now we gotta fight aliens.

Zombies and UFOs now officially exist. Crazy Carl knew. This is what he knew. He knew the aliens were real. He is prepared. Bless you Crazy Carl.

What is fascinating there are men who are angry they can't get hair cuts. They're upset they don't look like a young Harrison Ford or Brad Pitt during this apocalypse of aliens and zombies. They should man up, shave it off or let it grow out. They just need to face it, when it comes time to fight they're gonna look more like Randy Quaid. A hair cut ain't gonna save them.

Maybe the zombie illness will stop the aliens. I read about an illness stopping an alien invasion because of a virus. Maybe that'll work. I'm just not sure how to stop them yet.

But the zombies, well, I'm not going out that easy. They're just getting one in the head.

Then I'll sit out in front of my bunker, enjoy the scenery, and take a deep sip of my very black coffee.

Day 45

The kid wants to eat chips in her bunk. Fine, I told her. But she needed to do laundry. She said, she didn't know how to do laundry. I gave her the good news that her teacher called and said she was "gifted." Congrats!! You can learn laundry.

While on a ride around the neighborhood, a kid came running to us. Running so fast I thought she was zombie. She wanted to ride with us. I told her she couldn't we could be the zombies and she needed to go back to her bunker with her clan.

She was polite, but I didn't need some angry grandpa coming out from the bunker shooting first, and asking questions later. So we sent her back.

Because of all the biblical flooding my land looks like a jungle. The Godzilla snake has now probably brought friends--Like a T-Rex Turtle, or a Frankenstein Frog.

I'll probably need to borrow a flamethrower from

Crazy Carl to get through my yard. I wonder if he'll take coffee in trade.

Day 46

Holy F$%#&

I had this zombie attack all wrong!

ALL G$#@&^%$# WRONG!!

I've been planning for an attack from former humans. No! The attack is going to come from the zombie animals.

This morning I found, in what would have been referred to in the Time Before, two copperheads. They were in the bunker. They were ungodly huge.

But here's the thing, in The Time of Zombies, I cut off their heads--AND THEY STILL KEPT COMING.

Luckily Carl heard my screams of school girl terror and he came speeding over in his jeep, slammed on the breaks, jumped in the back, and fired up the flame-thrower and torched the zombie copperheads, bodies and heads. His face calm and still in the middle of the chaos.

After the flames and smoke died down, I thanked him. Offered him a bottle of whiskey. He took it. But then he surprised me, as he sat down next to me and began to eat charbroiled copperhead.

He offered me one. I declined, he had earned it--all of it. But we sat for a while eating and drinking in the midst of the smell of charbroiled zombie snake, smoke, and whiskey.

Then he turned to me and asked, "What do you want to kill tomorrow?"

Day 47

If this rain doesn't stop I'm going to need to machete this grass down. It's so wet, Crazy Carl's flamethrower couldn't do anything.

I did scope out the land. No current signed of zombie copperheads. But that doesn't mean they aren't there.

Not sure what the next step is, zombies, zombie snakes, UFOs. That's quite a to-do list. I miss old to do lists, pay electric bill, mow the lawn, bath the kid this month.

I planted some vegetables today. I just hope Zombie-Bambi does come for them.

Which raises the question, how does Zombie Bambi work, if you shoot the mom does she turn around and come back at you? Is that how that works?

I guess I'll find out here in a few weeks.

I'm sure Crazy Carl is ready to find out.

Day 48

Got the machete out and took down the zombie sized grass grown from the biblical sized floods--it took 14 hours.

Saw no Godzilla snake or Zombie snakes, but one can feel them watching--and waiting.

The problem with the Time of Zombies is the waiting. When are they going to attack? How are they going to attack? How much longer until the toilet paper is resupplied?

Crazy Carl was out digging in his land today. Not sure what he was digging--possibly a moat?

The-eight-year-old will need to clean her side of the bunker tomorrow. I may have better luck beating a hoard of zombie snakes than getting her to clean.

On that note, time to clean the sangria rations.

Day 49

The tally marks on the wall say day 49. It feels like 49 years.

Spent the day looking for zombie snakes. Didn't see any. I'm afraid they've developed camouflage.

People are going crazy. I see people without face-gear. Good look when the zombies try to rip your face off, but you left your face-gear at home--because it was hot.

I see some people are now concerned about "murder bees." Read the apocalypse--EVERYTHING WILL MURDER YOU. Please do try to keep up--and prepare accordingly.

Made the eight-year-old clean her side of the bunker. You would have thought I had asked her to eat zombie beets.

Thank goodness her teacher calls tomorrow.

Thank goodness there are Pop tarts. I can make it a few more tally marks.

Day 50

50 days. What the heck. That's a lot of tally marks on the wall.

50 days, does that make this the Golden Anniversary of the Apocalypse?

But what good is gold in the Apocalypse? It's too heavy to throw or use as a weapon, and certainly can't eat it. Now coffee, whiskey, toilet paper those things are valuable.

50 days--this is the Toilet Paper anniversary.

I saw tonight, in The Time Before would have been

referred to as a raccoon. As a self-studied zoologist of Zombie zoology, a raccoon will now be referred to as a Bear. I saw it on the southern part of the land, but I ain't worried. It's gotta get trough the Zombie snakes.

And Carl. I think Carl saw it. And Carl seems to like barbecued Zombie Raccoon-Bear. So I think I'm safe.

50 days--time to breakout the bourbon on the rocks.

.

Day 51

It rained. Again. Of course.

Read today of a more contagious form of zombie. I mean of course. It's only been a few days since the discovery of murder hornets, and a week since aliens. Something else needed to kill us.

I'm beginning to think we're not in the Apocalypse, but The Matrix. We're in a world wide simulation--a video game. The programmer is just upping the difficulty level to see how we do. Playing with us--laughing.

Now, the only question is who is "The One?" The One who can fight back against the architect?

Dear Lord, it can't be Crazy Carl.

I need a drink.

Day 52

It's colder than it should be. Zombies like the cold.

Didn't see any zombie hornets today. Or zombie-snakes.

So today was a good day.

But that can change in a zombie minute.

I wonder what will be discovered tomorrow that can kill us: A parasitic snake, manure hurricane, non-alcoholic whiskey...

Found a bike on the side of the road today. I don't want to describe what I found it next to...but he ain't gonna need it.

Now hopefully riding the bike won't kill me.

Day 53

Birthday in the bunker. The zombies stayed away--for today.

It's the first birthday in the bunker, but it seems like I've spent all the birthdays in the bunker.

Chocolate Cake is still possible to make in the confines of a bunker.

The kid and I have discover we need to where goggles when traveling by bike around the old neighborhood. Sand hits your eyes hard--put the goggles on.

Zombie virus also hits your face hard--put the face-gear on.

I noticed tonight while out in the neighborhood the tumbleweed seem to be growing thorns. Because of course they are.

Time for a birthday bourbon on the rocks.

Day 54

Guess what? It rained. Again. Today.

Also it's supposed to freeze tonight. What the
H$%^(

According to the tally marks on the wall, in The
Time Before this should be Spring.

We are not in the Apocalypse. We are in The Matrix. The programmer is playing us. Zombies, UFOs,
Murder Hornets,biblical floods, social distance, missing
toilet paper....

Hey! Pick one way to get rid of us and focus!

Watch!

I'm going to focus.

Pop Tarts and Sangria.

Focused.

Day 55

I have a plan for getting rich in The Time of Zombies.

1) Go to the market

2) Note people not wearing face-gear

3) Find out the location of their bunker

4) Wait

5) Claim their bunker

I'll go in with Crazy Carl on this. He wears a welders mask when out. He'll be fine.

The news is suppose to freeze tonight. That's perfect zombie weather. In The Time Before this was May. In the Time of Zombies, I'm beginning to wonder if the weather is like the old Game of Thrones books where seasons lasted for years.

Winter is Coming.

Maybe George RR Martin and Stephen King are running this Matrix.

Well it's cold. Time to check the whiskey rations.

Day 56

Still cold. Zombies still exist.

Crazy Carl had his welder's mask on outside of his bunker. He was welding something together in the front of his bunker. Looks like scaffolding. What is he making?

An antenna to talk to the aliens? A wall to keep out the Zombies? A two story flame thrower?

I stood and watched him while I sipped my coffee. Crazy Carl watching is my entertainment during this time.

Also sangria-- it's cold outside.

And Pop Tarts.

Day 57

Wow. 57 days. That's a lot of tally marks on the wall. I can't tell if feels like 57 minutes or 57 years. Time means nothing now.

Cleaned the bunker today. Not sure if needed cleaning, or if I was cleaning to keep my sanity. Probably both.

It's still cold. I could have sworn that in The Time Before this was May. Zombies like the cold. Maybe it's The Night King that's in charge of these Zombies.

Winter is Coming.

Crazy Carl didn't weld in the front yard today. But there was a lot of banging coming from his bunker.

His welding project had been moved indoors.

The kid asked what was he doing.

Who knows. At least his bunker isn't on fire or has exploded.

The kid's teacher called early today. The kid got all excited about a new early time.

Note to self, give kid more exciting things to do.

At least it didn't rain today. Not sure if it's safe come out of the Ark yet.

Which raises the question were Pop Tarts on the first Ark? They come in packages of two anyway.

I guess it's time to go eat a pair of Pop Tarts. Certainly can't eat just one and leave the other one lonely.

Day 58

It is still cold. Zombies flourish in this.

Trying to grow vegetables in the southern part of my land. Don't know if that is a smart thing to do. You just don't know what is going to come out of the ground. Will the zombie cucumbers have thrones, will zombie carrots be sharp as knives. Will zombie water-melons have whiskey in them? Actually that would be desirable--how do I make that happen?

Crazy Carl went back to welding today. I just stood and sipped my coffee as he added metal siding to the fifteen foot scaffolding he already had up. As long as he doesn't blow my bunker up, it's my morning entertainment.

He has large tractor tires set to the side. So that raises questions.

Like--Hey Carl! Where do you get tractor trailer tires during the apocalypse?

Some people at the market seem to think the zombies have gone away.

Cool. That's cool.

Can I lay claim to your bunker to store my Pop Tarts?

Day 59

Something's beginning to poke it's head up out of the ground in the garden. I just hope it's cucumbers and not the undead.

We rode around the neighborhood today. The tumbleweed is increasing. Riding bikes does make the vultures ignore us a little more--for now.

While sipping my morning coffee, seemed to be attached a flame thrower to whatever this contraption he has in his front yard. Makes me wonder what's on his "What to kill today" list.

Hopefully, it's the dragon ducks on my land. They're getting loud.

Oh, well,as long as he doesn't blow up my bunker.

Note to self, check fire extinguisher.

Maybe he'll be up for toasting some Pop Tarts.

Day 60

60 days Noah was sequestered in the ark for only 40. Clearly we have messed up.

60 days. That's a lot of tally marks. May need a new wall.

The zombies have won. My Pop Tart rations were low. But the market only had generic store made pop tarts. It's not the same. But a man's gotta eat.

While sipping my morning coffee, Crazy Carl was blasting classic rock today while welding. He must be in his flow. His flamethrower was in good voice today--reaching 40-50 feet.

Just as long as he doesn't blow my bunker up.

Now, what pairs with store brand pop tarts--I would recommend whiskey.

Day 61

61 days. That's two months of this mess.

It finally warmed up today. Crazy Carl seems to be working on a second flame thrower. Lot's of welding. He was playing Led Zepplin on the stereo.

Was that a grenade launcher I saw on the far side of his yard. Well as long as he doesn't blow up my bunker.

61 days. Not enough Pop Tarts for this nonsense.

But maybe there's enough Sangria.

Day 62

I don't know why I number the days. They're all the same.

Maybe recording the tally marks on the wall do help with a routine.

My new routine is sipping my morning coffee while Crazy Carl watching. This morning I saw an engine on his front lawn. "Going some where?" I pointed at the engine. He looked up at me, stared with his welders mask on and then went back to welding. He was playing Guns and Roses.

I hope I didn't just put myself on his "What to kill today" list.

Wore my face-gear to a bunker that was doing an old fashion yard sale. They weren't wearing face-gear and they seemed to be selling everything. They must be giving up, Not good. On the other hand, I now know where an empty bunker will be.

Sad news today--the sangria rations are low. Combine that with store brand Pop Tarts. Ugh.

A 62 day aged whiskey it is then.

Day 63

Saw what use to be called in The Time Before was called a deer. There were two. They looked very polite--until one stood up and aimed gun back at me. So I quietly went back into the bunker. They moved on a like a gang. Zombie-Deer.

Went back to the market to get proper Pop Tarts.

Crazy Carl played Free Bird from his bunker. I just sipped my coffee and wondered about the smoke coming from his bunker. But he never came out for me to ask. His welding project was still on the front lawn of the bunker.

I just hope he finishes his project before he blows up my bunker by accident.

Not going to worry about that right, I got my name brand Pop Tarts.

Day 64

Oh good. It rained. Again. Maybe I should only keep track of the non-rainy days.

Sipping my morning coffee, Crazy Carl was blasting Queen and I realized he was welding a boat--with tractor tires. An amphibious boat it looks like. Complete with gigantic flamethrowers. Float on the water--kill things on land.

And with all this rain the mosquitoes are now referred to as birds, and my backyard will be the home to several more dragon-ducks.

How did he know it was going to rain? Again?

Crazy Carl must be an alien. That can be the only explanation.

In The Time Before, I believe this would have been May. "April showers bring May flowers."

In the Time of Zombies, I believe the saying goes--"Showers today bring Showers tomorrow."

Ugh...I need whiskey today.

Day 65

It rained. Again. Zombies and Biblical Flooding, I didn't have that on my Apocalypse Bingo Board.

I missed my morning entertainment of seeing what Crazy Carl was doing, because the rain. But I'm pretty certain I heard The Rolling Stones coming from his bunker. So I sipped my morning coffee listening to Mick and the sound of banging.

The eight-year-old doesn't seem to care about the Apocalypse, as long as her teacher calls her everyday, we're all good. Unfortunately she then watches videos of other people playing video games. Video games she has. Video games she could be playing at that moment. But no, let's spend the Apocalypse watching someone ELSE play video games.

I need to get Crazy Carl over here so we can take her zombie hunting. Stop watching other people play video games. Stop playing video games. BE the video game.

Oh look, a Great White Catfish just swam by the bunker. Maybe I'll grab a whiskey and watch Jaws to remember a time when sharks were smaller.

To quote Quint:

I had a little drink about an hour ago and it got right to my head / Wherever I may roam / by land or sea or foam...

Day 66

The 66th day. It rained. Again. For the 4 millionth time. It is also cold. In The Time Before, if my count is correct, this would be late May. This isn't Time Before Weather. This is Zombie weather.

Crazy Carl took the day off. I think the weather even depressed him. So I sipped my morning coffee in silence, Until the Pterodactyl Owls began hooting.

This was also the time I realized my coffee rations need attention. Nothing gets done without coffee. No coffee, no Pop Tart, whiskey, or sangria time later. It all begins with coffee. Focus your supplies there.

We ventured out briefly, during the 7 minute 37 second break in the rain. Didn't see vultures, the clouds were too low--Or they were also home depressed. But we did see what used to be referred to as earthworms. But I don't know if we should call them worms anymore. Based on what I saw--I think Subterranean Carnivorous Eels are a more appropriate term.

I began this 66th day sipping coffee. I'll need to finish it nursing a whiskey.

Day 67

It rained. Today. Not sure how Noah handled this. Oh, yeah he released a Dove. But if I release a dove, it will get eaten by a Pterodactyl Owl or torched by a Dragon Duck. Maybe I need to sacrifice a box of Pop Tarts. Well, that's just going too far.

Crazy Carl had his garage open, there were banging noises of varied pitch and rhythm. I believe it was Aerosmith coming from the speakers.

I thinking taking up fishing. I'll start with some subterranean carnivorous eels as bait, and we'll good hunt for the Great White Catfish I keep seeing swim near the bunker. He is beginning to task me, I think.

I didn't replenish my coffee rations. Not smart to be pushing the coffee rations. No coffee, no Crazy Carl watching, no zombie zoology study...it all starts with the coffee. Focus there.

But due to the rain, it ends with whiskey.

Day 68

Wait. It was sunny today. I didn't send a dove after the rain stopped. I want to be excited, but I've learned not to trust.

The kid and I went around the neighborhood several times today. We see more vultures than we do stray kids. I hope that's because they're safe in their bunker and not because they've been eaten.

It's rained so much the tumbleweed made damp splashing sounds as they blew across the road.

While walking the canine later, I did see two stray kids, but they kept their distance.

I continue to see The Great White Catfish that is swimming in what used to be a stream on the southern part of my land, but is now almost a lake. If he causes too much trouble, I may need a bigger boat. Crazy Carl has a bigger boat. I wonder how much whiskey or pop tarts rations that will cost me.

The kid has gone to bed. Since it's nice weather for the first time in many moons, I'll just have a cold beer.

Day 69

69 Days. Which means one month until 100 days. Ugh. It already feels like a 100 days.

Spent the day cleaning the bunker. Every inch felt like a victory. The kid wanted something extra for the extra chore of cleaning the windows. I gave her half a Pop Tart.

I think I'm seeing or better yet, hearing a new type of bird. The kid said it was the bush sneezing. No the bush wasn't sneezing, I could have sworn it was a bird. But then again, all bets are off, and it could be the bush was actually sneezing. Which means now I have to look out for plants.

Speaking of plants.we have cucumbers, carrots, and watermelons coming up in the garden. At least I hope it's cucumbers, carrots, and watermelons, and not something else. What exactly would a zombie cucumber be or do?

Apparently it was Crazy Carl's mom birthday. So

he decided to light up his flamethrower in celebration. Gotta find that fire extinguisher tomorrow.

Because it was the second day of no rain, the kid and I rode around the neighborhood. We saw no other kids. I am concerned.

The coffee rations were refilled. And for a brief moment. All was right with the world.

Day 70

70 days, what the heck, that's a lot of Pop Tarts. Feels like 70 years.

The King Kong Ground Hog was back. I saw it poke his head up out of the ground, but he was in back of Crazy Carl's backyard. That's a brave ground hog.

Crazy Carl wasn't out today. And I didn't hear classic rock coming from his bunker today. Maybe it was the dreary weather.

No rain, but cold and gray. By my count, it's late May. The Zombies are winning.

I saw two roses buds blooming on my land. I am afraid to touch them--afraid they may bite back. Like that plant in Little Shop of Horrors. Zombie-plants the new normal. The new normal--Vegans don't eat plants, plants eat vegans.

Speaking of plants, I tried out a blueberry wine tonight. Expanding the possibilities for the bunker. Hope the sangria doesn't get jealous.

I watched the Great White Catfish swim by the bunker again I sure hope the water goes down soon--or I'm gonna need to borrow Carl's boat.

Time for a nightcap, Pop Tarts with whiskey.

New idea for a Pop Tart flavor, Brown Sugar Whiskey.

Day 71

No rain today. Amazing.

I spent my morning sipping coffee and watching Crazy Carl welding again. Today's selection was Led Zeppelin. Zeppelin 2 if memory serves. It looks like he is building a metal pirate ship that also has tractor wheels--plus a flamethrower on top. I just hope he doesn't blow my bunker up.

My question is weather the thing will float. The water to the south of our lands is still filled with water-and the Great White Catfish. I'll wait to see how he gets it there.

Maybe if I trade some whiskey he'll give me an old flamethrower.

Started the day off with coffee, time to wrap it up with a nice pairing of Pop Tarts and sangria.

Day 72

Very cloudy today. No rain. But no real sun either. Make up your mind weather.

But with the lack of rain, the kid and I did travel a couple of times around the area. I did see one child free from their bunker. Still concerned about the others. Especially when I see the vultures above.

The kid's teacher said this would be the last week she would be calling. What incoming fresh hell is this? Please keep calling we need you. Pop tarts? Sangria? Whiskey? Crazy Carl's flame thrower. Name your price teacher!

I have to fight zombies AND teach the kid! Well, the kid needs to learn how to throw the Holy Hand Grenade of Antioch anyway.

To add to my misery I saw Crazy Carl working without his shirt on, while Free Bird played from the speakers.

The was no warning for that.

I need a drink.

Day 73

73. That's one day for each home run Barry Bonds hit while juiced. I pray to the Good Lord we are not dealing with this for the total number of home runs Juiced Bonds hit over his total career--762.

I sipped my morning coffee while Crazy Carl blared Aerosmith and Run DMC and he went back to full on welding--Not a quiet morning.

This thing in front of his bunker does look like something I was expecting from the Apocalypse--it's metal, large, massive tires, and clearly gets 1 to 2 miles per gallon. He also seems to have added a crow's nest, like on old pirate ships. What does that long gray haired classic rock blaring guy know? Is he preparing for the Second Wave.

This afternoon I could have sworn I saw a penguin in the trees behind the bunker. It was black, white and seemed to waddle, but then swam across the pond. Did the zombie virus reach Antarctica? What does a zombie penguin do? I would have thought the Dragon Ducks would have done something about a Zombie Penguin? I have so much to learn about this new zoology.

The Great White Catfish didn't seem to be interested in whatever it was. But it's beady black eyes definitely seemed to be interested in me.

At least Crazy Carl goes to bed early, I can enjoy my Sangria in peace.

Day 74

Oh hey--Look it rained. I forgot what rain looked like. How I've missed it so.

I sure hope Crazy Carl's metal ark floats.

The rain kept me from having my morning coffee from watching Crazy Carl weld and play classic rock. Instead it was just me and the canine.

The cucumbers, carrots, and watermelons are coming up fast, Zombie rain seems to have extra fertilizer ability. I just hope King Kong Ground Hog leaves them alone.

I keep eyeing the Great White Catfish in the pond-- we may need a bigger bunker.

The kids teacher said she would only be calling a couple of more times. Please teacher don't leave! I know a guy--I can hook you up on a good deal on Pop Tarts.

Or sangria--cases of it. Just please keep calling the kid!

Here's to you teacher, this whiskey's for you.

Day 75

75 Days. What the heck. Three quarters of the way to a hundred days. That's a lot of tally marks on the wall. Gonna need a new wall soon.

Sipping my morning coffee--Italian Roast--I watched Crazy Carl begin putting the tractor tires on his Frankenstein vehicle. Steely Dan seemed to be today's choice in music. Still not 100% sure how this two story metal monstrosity is supposed to move. I am 100% confident in it's ability to burn things down. Just hope it's not my bunker he burns down.

The kid and I were out in the afternoon, we actually saw another kid out. I was relieve to know not all the kids had been eaten.

It was good to see more people out with their face-gear on. Not sure why it took 75 days of zombies for them to get there.

Noticed some rosebuds today. Went to take a look and the plant slapped me with the thorns. Zombie-Rose should have seen that coming. i just hope the Zombie-Rose stays in the ground and doesn't become mobile. I just don't think I could handle mobile Zombie-Rose bushes.

I realized this afternoon, the Pop Tart rations need attending to. I will put the face-gear next to the door to make a trip to the market tomorrow.

Luckily the sangria rations are fine...for now.

Day 76

G$%$**^ saw a Zombie Snake again today! Trying to have a nice a bike ride--me and the kid--and a G^%&(($ Zombie-snake right there in front of us. Thank goodness our bikes work.

And no Crazy Carl around!

Thanks to the Good Lord we made it.

Later in the afternoon, the kid made a visit with a friend. Thank goodness that kid hasn't been eaten by zombies. We would be in real trouble then. No teacher, no friend. Ugh.

Noticed the watermelon are coming up. I sure hope they're normal. Maybe Zombie-Watermelons just spit their seeds at you before you eat them.

Still thinking about that G%$##$#@& Zombie-snake, where's the whiskey?

Day 77

77 days. Ugh gonna need a new wall--so many tally marks.

Crazy Carl was quiet today. No classic rock to wake up to. I wonder what he does on these days in his bunker. I imagine he's on an old short-wave radio talking to aliens.

So instead, I just sipped my coffee with the Zombie-Roses, Dragon Ducks, and Pterodactyl Owls.

Apparently whiskey is now sparse in the area. Looking at my rations, I maybe wealthier than I realize.

And I resupplied the Pop Tart rations, so that's a good way to end the day.

.

Day 78

The weather has actually been pleasant. I am afraid to write that. Who knows what weather will happen next.

Crazy Carl was back welding this morning. Listening to The Beetles Revolution album. I think he's adding a third flamethrower, and one of those, I think they're called cow catchers. They go on the front of old locomotives from the 1800s. This thing is going to take a lot of diesel.

Something ate the buds off my zombie-roses. I am concerned about what sort of animal that is able to do that. They have to get past the thorns and still be able to swallow the poisonous bud. That's concerning.

There was some crazy man yelling at clouds today. I guess we all have something to yell at these days. I just hope he's not a zombie.

Day 79

No rain. Dare I continue to hope for continued good weather?

Sipping my morning coffee, I realized Crazy Carl was playing Alanis Morissette. Ironic choice for Carl--I think. He seemed to finally put on all four wheels onto this two story metal contraption. It has a cow catcher on front, three flame throwers on the first deck. A captain bridge, where I guess he drives this thing, on top of that is the crows nest. Where I guess he can look for Moby Dick when he's out on the water. This thing is either going to be epic or nothing.

Something is eating my flowers. I don't want to be one of those crazy people that guards their flowers. But I think I'm headed down that road. I need to find this squirrel if that is what it is.

It's a nice warm night, sangria it is then.

Day 80

80 days. That's twice as long as Noah was in the ark or Jesus was in the desert. Clearly, we have messed up.

But Crazy Carl has not messed up, his darn contraption actually went down the street and back today. It actually made me pause sipping my coffee. I stood there mid-sip as it blew black smoke from the stern of the ship. He was even gracious enough to test out the flames throwers. They work.

Note to self, get two more back up fire extinguishers and install a sprinkler system.

He shouted over the diesel engine and Guns and Roses, that he would put it in the water tomorrow. But first he needed to fix the aliment since it pulled "port side."

Question, on vehicles that are driven on land, wouldn't port side, just be left? Second note to self, don't actually ask him that.

The Apocalypse so far doesn't look like the Mad Max world. I had imagined, but don't worry, Crazy Carl is gonna get us there.

Time for some Pop Tarts and in honor of Crazy Carl, I'm gonna toast them.

Day 81

It was hot. Like actually hot. Desert hot.

It's hard to wear the face-gear in the hot. But the zombies still exist so the face-gear remains on.

Zombie squirrels seem be leaving my flowers and gardens alone for the moment. Not sure how to keep them from coming back.

Crazy Carl drove his two story metal contraption around the back of his bunker to the lake that is still there from the weeks of rain. I sipped my coffee and watched him as the contraption slowly made it's way into the water, to the sound track of Led Zeppelin. It jerked as it he slowed it down into the water. And holy cow it floated. Black smoke came out of the smoke stack, as it crept across the new lake.

Holy crap he did it.

Carl is coming for you Zombies.

I raise a glass of whiskey to you sir.

Day 82

Again. Hot. Like I need the pool hot. But no pool. Zombies.

Crazy Carl did not come out of his bunker today. So I was alone sipping my morning coffee. Sometimes I appreciate when he is quiet and stays in the bunker. And then there are days I am scared that was quiet in his bunker. Today I was scared.

What does he know?

Consequently spent a lot of the day cleaning the bunker. Apparently the kid as become an artist. I found green globs on the floor by her bathroom. I am going to be positive and assume it was paint and not alien blood. But then again with my luck...

Replenished the Pop Tart rations and if my counting is right this would be a Friday. In The Time Before, we has a saying it's five o'clock somewhere--thus we can drink adult beverages.

But in the Time of Zombies, it's five o'clock all the time--time means nothing.

So on that note I'll celebrate a quiet Crazy Carl with a nice blueberry wine, it pairs well with Frost Brown Sugar Cinnamon.

Day 83

It's hot. It's muggy. Last night a thunderstorm nearly knocked the bunker over. Even the weather has become Zombiefied.

Tomorrow I am supposed to get the stuff that keeps zombie-deer from eating my plants. I wonder if will be nightshade or cyanide capsules.

Sipping my morning coffee, I watched Crazy Carl drive his machine from his bunker down the street--today's soundtrack Bowie's Under Pressure. Lots of people came out their bunkers to watch the parade of a crazy man and his Frankenstein vehicle. Crazy Carl still hasn't come back as of yet. Not sure what to make of that.

The dragon-ducks were getting loud tonight. Maybe they know if another zombie thunderstorm is coming--or maybe they were complaining about the heat.

The bunker is humid tonight. Let's hope this sangria will help me sleep.

Day 84

Not as hot today. Or maybe I'm just getting used to it. At least it's not flooding.

I think the Great White Catfish is getting nervous about his new lake. Can catfish walk across the ground. In The Time Before I knew of certain species of catfish that could leave one pond and cross over to another body of water. That Zombie Catfish can probably walk--because zombies.

The spray stuff to stop the zombie-deer from eating the plants came today. It smelled like mint, which is not what I was expecting.

Went to the market today, more people wearing face-gear. Which is good. But some people don't seem to know how to wear them. If I can see your nostrils-- you're not wearing the face-gear correctly.

Sipping my coffee this morning Crazy Carl came out of his bunker. Without his two story vehicle. I didn't ask where he had been yesterday. But I watched him dump ashes behind his bunker. Like a large trash can of ashes. Did he get something with the flame-throwers? If he did, why keep the ashes? I have questions.

If my math is correct in The Time Before, this would be Sunday. So Sangria it is then.

Day 85

85. That's only fifteen more til 100. Ugh.

Apparently it was the King Kong Groundhog eating the flowers and not the Zombie-deer. Or least I saw the King Kong Ground Hog. So he's back. I wonder if he's brought the Godzilla Snake.

The kid caught a toad tonight, first thing that hasn't looked like a zombie in a while--expect it didn't want to jump out of her hands. Didn't they use to want to jump out of your hands? Hope she's not a Zombie now.

I'm sad this is the last week the kid's teacher will call. Why is everything awful?

Please teacher please keep calling, whisky, sangria, Pop tarts. You name it. Just keep calling the kid.

Day 86

Crazy Carl was quiet today. I am concerned.

The Great White Catfish is staring at me as it's small pond is slowly shrinking to back to normal. I may need to steal Crazy Carl's metal boat and take this Great White Catfish out. He tasks me.

The amount of frogs and toads around here is concerning. It's like a plague. Screw it, might as well throw in a plague as well.

Went to the market today, to review, IF I can SEE your Nostrils your face-gear isn't working.

Due to all the nostrils I saw I forgot to replenish the Pop Tart rations. Ugh...

We'll see how chocolate chip cookies pair with a nice whiskey.

Day 86-Part 2

86 days. Two weeks until 100 days. What the heck. That will be a ton of tally marks on the wall.

The cucumbers, watermelons, and carrots seem to be coming in. The weeds seem quicker to come in now, as opposed in The Time Before. Zombie-weeds.

The Great White Catfish swam back and forth in his shrinking pond, watching me as I weeded.

I am curious as to what a zombie-cucumber will do. Will be extra prickly in the skin? Will it be tough to peel? Will it eat you with ranch?

I am concerned people seem to think the zombies have gone away. They have not. Zombies don't care that you're bored. In fact, maybe they want you bored. That way they can grab you on the way to your cookout. The zombies are always waiting.

Found a zombie-toad on the outside wall of the bunker tonight. The kid thought it was cute. It won't be so cute when it jumps down on top of us and grabs us by the neck. Note to self--borrow flamer thrower from Crazy Carl.

Didn't see Crazy Carl today. He knows to hide from the zombies. But clearly he is prepared from when a full head-on attack is need. But even he knows your first priority is to not be seen.

Forgot to replenish the Pop Tarts today. I hope I'm not a Zombie and am forgetting important things.

I still have sangria, so I'm good.

Day 87

Dreary day. Humid as well. Apparently it's supposed to start raining again in the next of couple days-- because of course it is.

I am sure the Great White Catfish will be happy for that. He keeps staring at me when I am out behind the bunker.

I am sure Crazy Carl will be more than ready for the next flood. He was working on something in his bunker today. The garage door was open and there was the sound of hammering and banging and Aerosmith. I wonder what his next project is. Maybe an airplane?

The kid told me today that tomorrow is the last day her teacher will be calling. Please teacher don't go! Why is everything awful?

Where's the whiskey...

Day 88

Nice weather around here. Of course it's going to rain soon. I think that's why the Great White Catfish smiled at me today. He knows that soon he can get closer. I could have sworn I saw him poke his head out of the water and put a fin on dry land.

The watermelon plants seem to be coming in nicely, but the weeds are definitely zombie-weeds. They haven't killed the watermelons, but they've gotten most of the carrots. But it seems the cucumbers are actually fighting back against the zombie-weeds. That should be a new area of study, which vegetables kill zombie-weeds.

Crazy Carl was yelling at someone today. Didn't look like a zombie to me. But he went inside got his flamethrower and sent him running off his property. Note to self --don't piss Crazy Carl off.

The kid and I went walking and we ran into another zombie-snake, because of course we do. I ran it off, and someone else asked if was a snake, the kid said yes, but not a big one. She's grown used to the snakes here in The Time of Zombies.

The Apocalypse is truly here. The kids teacher said today was the last day for them meeting. The kid was very upset. Teacher, please, whiskey, sangria, bourbon, pop tarts, flamethrower--tell me your price--just call the kid.

See I have nice vintage of bourbon. I have a whole case. Just call the kid.

Day 89

The Great White Catfish made it a few feet past the water today. I knew of some catfish that could walk on water in The Time Before. But I've never seen it in person. He made a few steps out, breathed a little and then turned around back into the water. He turned and looked me with his beady black eyes. I'm gonna need Crazy's Carl's boat.

Speaking of Crazy Carl, he hasn't driven his diesel powered amphibious boat in a few days. I sure hope it still works. I heard him banging on something to-day--David Bowie was his sound track today.

The kid visited a friends today. One of the few I know not to be a zombie. Get her out of the bunker more often I say.

I heard someone setting off fireworks tonight. Have the zombies been defeated or was it a battle that I missed. i don't think the zombies have been defeated yet. Just wear your facegear.

Tonight's selection is a nice blueberry wine, goes well with chocolate chip cookies.

Day 90

90 days. Three months. Ten more days until 100. That's a lot of tally marks on the wall. Probably going to need to start on a new wall soon.

By my count, in The Time Before, it was a Sunday. The Lord's Day, so I spent some time cleaning and fixing up the bunker. Every inch clean is a victory.

Crazy Carl took his metal amphibious vehicle out. He took it to the back of his property to his new pond and he drove it in. He turned off the diesel engine and just floated. He sat down on a chair and got out a fishing pole. I sipped my coffee and watched. He didn't catch a thing. But to enjoy the Apocalypse in a metal boat, while fishing seems to be not a bad way to spend Zombie Time.

The kid and I went out riding. She's good about wearing her face-gear. Some other people are not wearing their face-gear. Or maybe they're already zombies, and don't need the face-gear.

The Great White Catfish was still staring at me this afternoon. I'm gonna need to pay Crazy Carl with some whiskey rations to get rid of this white whale of mine.

Tonight I'll just stare it down, while I drink a bourbon.

Day 91

Oh look it's raining. Tomorrow it will rain. The day after that it will rain. God's wrath took a couple of days off--but it's back.

The Great White Catfish, I swear winked at me and smiled. Then he decided to try two front fins on the ground, before he turned back around into the water.

I sipped my morning coffee wondering why Crazy Carl wasn't out in his boat. Now seemed a perfect time. Maybe he's just waiting for another day or two. His boat was really built for Noah like conditions anyway. Or the desert of the Egyptians, either environment will work for his boat. It's marvelous actually--the perfect

Apocalypse Vehicle.

The rain will also mean the Dragon Ducks will be back. They make a lot of noise--and fire.

On a good note, I replenished the Pop Tart rations. They're the perfect rainy weather food--The Perfect Apocalypse Food.

Day 92

Oh look rain. How I've missed it since...yesterday.

92 days. I think maybe 12 have been dry.

The Great White Catfish was happy. He swam back and forth from one of his pond to the other. I watched him from the back of the bunker as I sipped my coffee. He seems larger. Note to self: find a harpoon.

Speaking of harpoons, Crazy Carl had his two story

boat out today. He was welding on a canopy over a part of the deck. Even Crazy Carl wants to remain dry. He tested out the flamethrowers in the rain. They work.

The kid's teacher didn't call today or yesterday. She's really gone. The kid seems fine. Watched a lot of Adventure TIme and Teen Titans. Then felt the need to paint crafts. So not bad. Asked the kid if she wanted a different different teacher to call her this summer. She said, "Summer school?! No."

I may sign her up anyway.

Went to the market today. Many many many people seem confused about how to use the face-gear. If I can see your nose, you didn't put it on correctly.

Face-gear is similar to pants, if I can see your butt, your pants aren't on correctly. Any people will be confused as to why they became zombies.

It's raining. I need warm sunny weather. So sangria it is.

Day 93

93 days. Three months of Zombies. One week until 100 days. What the heck. It feels like a 100 years.

It rained. Again. Crazy Carl should have built an ark. He seems to talk to the Big Guy Upstairs. What does he know?

The Great White Catfish is getting closer to the bunker. He seems bolder now. Taking several steps outside of the pond onto the grass. Gonna need a harpoon. Hopefully Crazy Carl's boat is named the Pequod.

It's extraordinary how many people don't realize that the face-gear goes over the nose. The nose.

Luckily ice cream still exists in the market. Will need to up the rations as the kid is eating through our new ice cream rations in this warming weather.

Sangria luckily pairs nicely with an ice cream cone.

Day 94

Well. Miracles happen. It didn't rain today. I've said it before it. It would be less work to just record the non-rainy days.

Which meant luckily the kid and I could get out around the neighborhood. Not seeing many kids around the neighborhood, concerned the zombies got them.

I saw the Great White Catfish leave the water behind the bunker today and make it a good ten feet to the bunker. It's teeth sharp. It dragged itself by it's whiskers, and wiggled it's way toward the bunker. It's white skin glistened in the afternoon sun. It took deep gasps as it stared at the bunker. I grabbed a baseball bat. Not sure exactly how to kill a ten-foot zombie catfish. But as it stared at me it turned back to the water. Ahab would be nervous.

People assume zombies are gone. I'll show them my great fish and prove them wrong.

The Great White Catfish is leaving the watermelons, carrots, and cucumbers alone. Unlike the rose bushes, the watermelon vines leave me alone. Maybe they're not zombies, one of the few things on my property--not zombie.

I did see King Kong Groundhog today. He's at least leaving the garden alone. And unlike the great fish, the ground hog keeps his distance.

It's getting warmer--summer. Thinking about switching to rum--and coconut. What does a zombie coconut do?

Day 95

95. 95 days. More than three months. Five days to a hundred. That's a lot of tally marks.

Some people don't believe the zombies exist. Despite them being right there in their neighborhood, in the market, in the gym. Mind boggling.

Crazy Carl drove his amphibious boat into the neighborhood today, Ramble On by Zepplin was his soundtrack. The boat starts off slow and then the diesel engine finds its life and it begins tolling at a full steam of 25 miles per hour.

I wonder where he went to. He spent the whole day out. I just heard him come back in. I wonder what he was up to the whole day out. Some sort of banging is coming from his garage right now.

The Great White Catfish pulled it's way out of the pond this afternoon. The canine was barking to let me know. I went outside with the baseball bat and grabbed a garden hoe. He's slow on the ground, But his fins can hurt. And his whiskers will reach out and get you. That's where the garden hoe comes in. But the mud kept him from getting any closer and he slid back into the pond. Repeated note to self: find harpoon.

If my math is correct it would be a Friday night in The Time Before, pop tarts and a beer it is then.

Day 96

96 days. 4 days until 100. 96 days...just wow.

That's a lot of tally marks. Luckily it didn't really rain today. I think even rain is tired of rain.

Sipping my morning coffee I watched Crazy Carl begin digging in the front of his bunker. He was using a regular shovel, I would have thought he would be using something more machine, something more diesel powered. But alas he just dug all morning in the front of his bunker.

The Great White Catfish stayed in the pond today. But he eyed me as i weeded the garden. His dorsal fin going back and forth over the water.

King Kong Ground Hog is getting closer and more comfortable. I am afraid he may have discovered the garden.

I have grown so jaded that while walking the canine, a zombie-snake slithered through the grass near us, and I didn't flinch. In The Time Before I would have screamed like a four year old girl.

If my math is correct, today is the start of summer. But really who keeps track of time anymore.

Except Pop Tart time, I always keep track of that. And it is that time.

Day 97

97 days. Maybe one day historian will find this, and lament, "Poor sucker he has no idea just how many more days he has..."

A miracle happened today. It didn't rain. I was afraid to venture out and enjoy the nice weather. Still few to no other kids in the area. I'm concerned.

The canine barked at a zombie-deer this morning. I could have sworn the the deer stood up on it's hind legs and took off. I guess I should consider myself lucky that the zombie-deer didn't turn around and come at us.

Later sipping my morning coffee, Crazy Carl continued digging in the front of his bunker at first with just a regular shove. Lots of swear words as he worked. After about 30 minutes of that he went back into his bunker and came out with something more like I would have expected--a small bulldozer. Where does he get these things? After another 30 minutes, and another cup of coffee for me, he dug the hole around the sides of his bunker. Then he got out and went inside and stayed there for the rest of the day.

Went back to the market today, still confused at how people don't get that the face-gear goes over the nose. The nose.

It's a summer evening, that's a nice pairing with a sangria.

Day 98

Wow, the day after tomorrow is 100 days, That's a lot of tally marks.

Rain was back today. Along with hail, wind, and lightning. Zombie summer weather.

Sipping my morning coffee I noticed Crazy Carl had lined the hole in front of his bunker with concrete. All that's missing is water, and he has a moat. Wait, he's making a moat.

Wonder how much he charges to install one of those?

That would make a good business now in The Time of Zombies--moat installations.

The Great White Catfish crawled further out today during the hail storm and dark skies overhead. I swear he seemed to roar when it thundered. I didn't dare go outside, no point in getting hit by lightning while carrying a metal baseball bat.

What pairs with 98 days. A nice bourbon I believe.

Day 99

99 days. The wall is full of tally marks. Gonna need to find a new wall.

No rain today. The weather was actually mildly summer like.

Sipping my morning coffee I watched Crazy Carl beginning to fill in his moat. He created a new door that comes out of his bunker it's big enough for his diesel amphibious boat. His soundtrack was Zepplin while he filled the moat.

The Great White Catfish made climbed out of the pond today. I grabbed a shovel and swung at some of his barbels. He didn't like that. But if he keeps doing this--I'm gonna need a bigger shovel.

Noticed today the carrots seem to be coming in nicely. I wonder if a zombie-carrot I can use as a harpoon against the Great White Catfish. And it looks like the cucumber and watermelon are also coming in fine. It looks like the anti-zombie spray seems to have worked. The garden has since been left alone.

It sounds like Crazy Carl just turned off the water at his bunker. I'm guessing he's finished his moat.

I guess I'll grab a beer and go see the results.

Day 100

100 days. Dear Lord in Heaven. Going to have to start recording tally marks on the other side of the wall. How many more days. The zombies are still here. Some people don't believe they are.

But they are.

Didn't rain today either. Interesting that I am recording whether or not it rained. It seems that maybe 17 days of the past 100 didn't have rain.

Crazy Carl did finish his moat last night. And he finished the draw bridge. It was a loud night. Deep Purple and Motorhead was his soundtrack.

The more interesting thing happened as I was sipping my morning coffee, watching this medieval architecture happen in front of me, was when the Great White Catfish came around in between out bunkers. I always thought he only came out when he saw me.

He pulled himself by the barbels and by flopping from side to side. His teeth sparkled in the sunlight.

I spilt my coffee. Crazy Carl though grabbed a chain. He has them hanging around in his bunker. He walked calmly over lassoed the great fish by the neck. He pulled it towards his bunker. The fish wasn't happy and tried slapping him with its barbels. Crazy Carl did swatted them away with his knife. He dropped the great fish into his moat.

"Now stay there!" he shouted. The water splashed violently. I felt some hit me.

The rest of the day Crazy Carl put up a fence around the moat--keeping the fish from climbing out. Not sure how long that will work.

But for right now, I'll a Pop Tart and some sangria and enjoy watching the Great White Catfish swimming in Crazy Carl's moat.

About the author

Martin Tiller is an elementary school teacher in Richmond, Virgini. He was taken off guard at how his silly Apocalypse journal posts connected with people. So he collected them.

He is also the author of The Dolbin School series, The Kevin Books Series, and The Number Invesigators. He can be found at martintillerauthor.com and Martin Tiller Author on Facebook.